THE
SUPERMARKET
GHOST

D0532891

Gordon Snell has written many books for children, as well as stage and radio comedy for children and adults, and books of verse including the popular *Rhyming Irish Cookbook*. He lives in Dublin with his wife, the best-selling author Maeve Binchy.

THE
SUPERMARKET
GHOST

Gordon Snell

Illustrator: Bob Byrne

THE O'BRIEN PRESS
DUBLIN

First published 2007 by The O'Brien Press Ltd,
12 Terenure Road East, Rathgar, Dublin 6, Ireland.
Tel: +353 1 4923333; Fax: +353 1 4922777
E-mail: books@obrien.ie
Website: www.obrien.ie

ISBN: 978-1-84717-049-1

Text © copyright Gordon Snell 2007
Copyright for typesetting, layout, editing, design
© The O'Brien Press Ltd

All rights reserved. No part of this publication may be reproduced
or utilised in any form or by any means, electronic or mechanical,
including photocopying, recording or in any information storage
and retrieval system, without permission in writing
from the publisher

British Library Cataloguing-in-Publication Data
A catalogue reference for this title is available from the British Library

1 2 3 4 5 6 7 8
07 08 09 10 11 12

The O'Brien Press receives
assistance from

Illustrations: Bob Byrne
Layout and design: The O'Brien Press Ltd
Printed and bound in the UK by J.H. Haynes & Co Ltd, Sparkford

For dearest Maeve, with all my love

CHAPTER ONE

The day Maria O'Malley first saw Davy had begun like an ordinary day. She was with her father, Mike, as he carried the big wooden tray of fresh loaves into the shop. It was the first week of the summer holidays and Maria had agreed to help her dad with his deliveries. She knew that her parents thought that she'd be bored around the house – summer camp wasn't starting for another two weeks. Maria enjoyed helping her dad, but she didn't like going into Paddy Breen's supermarket. Her dad had told her to cheer up, so Maria put on an eager smile as she walked beside him towards the shelves. Maria was wearing a t-shirt, three-quarter length jeans and new trainers.

'That smells good, Mike,' said Paddy Breen,

the supermarket manager.

'Baked this morning as usual,' said Mike O'Malley. Paddy called it a supermarket, though it was not really big enough to deserve the name. It had four central rows of shelves, as well as shelves at the side and back, and only one check-out counter near the door. Paddy's assistant, Rose, worked on the check-out. Rose acted like a princess and was more interested in her appearance than serving customers. Her hair was scraped back in a pony tail, and she always wore large, silver hoop earrings. Rose loved reapplying lip gloss and admiring her reflection.

Paddy Breen liked to think of himself as a big man in the town. He was on the council. He also owned a small garage and a number of houses that he rented out. He was a tall man with a round belly that stretched the jacket of the brown tweed suit he always wore. He was balding, with sandy-coloured hair and a rugged face. Paddy looked down at Maria as she followed her father into the store.

'I see you've brought your little helper with you today, Mike.' he said.

'I wouldn't be without her,' said Maria's father.

They went in, and he began to stack the loaves on to the empty shelves.

'Wait here, Maria, while I get another tray from the van,' said her father.

Maria gazed at the shelves along the back of the shop. There were lots of bags of flour: cream flour, baking flour, self-raising flour ... She wondered why there were so many different kinds. Maria was busy looking at her new trainers and twirling her plastic bracelet when she suddenly noticed a boy about her own age. He was wearing a dark-blue sweater, fraying at the sleeves, and he had long, scruffy fair hair. He smiled, and began running his hand along the bags of flour in front of him. Maria hadn't seen him before. Perhaps he was Paddy Breen's nephew helping to stack the shelves, she thought. The boy was pointing at one of the bags of flour, and then at Maria. Then he beckoned to her.

'What's up?' Maria asked, going across to him.

He pointed to the bag of flour again, and then held out his hands.

Maria was annoyed.

'Can't you get it down for yourself?' she asked.

The boy didn't answer. He put a finger to his lips in a hushing gesture. Perhaps he was a bit dim, she thought. So with a shrug, she took the bag of flour from the shelf and put it into his hands. It seemed to fall right through them. It landed with a thud and split open, spilling the flour on the floor.

'You clumsy eejit!' said Maria.

The boy didn't seem to care. He just stood there and put his hands on his hips and grinned at her. Maria thought that he really couldn't be right in the head.

'Aren't you going to clear it up?' she asked. 'Mr Breen will blow his top. Here, I'll help you, before he sees.'

She knelt down and began to scoop the spilt flour towards the bag with her hand. The boy didn't move. As Maria looked closer she noticed that his feet were bare.

'What's going on?' Paddy Breen appeared, followed by Maria's father carrying another tray of loaves. They both looked at Maria and the bag of spilt flour on the floor.

'Look at that!' said Paddy Breen. 'Kids! You can't leave them alone for five minutes. Get a dustpan and brush from Rose at the cash-desk, and clear it up.'

'There's no need to talk to my daughter like that,' said Maria's father. 'I'm sure it was just an accident.'

'She shouldn't have been messing around with the shelves.'

'But I wasn't,' said Maria, 'it wasn't my fault.'

'Well, whose fault was it, then?' Paddy Breen sneered.

'It was that boy. I handed the bag to him and he dropped it,' Maria said, turning around to show them the boy.

'What boy, Maria?' asked her father.

'Him!' she said, pointing, but the boy wasn't there.

'There's been no one else in the shop since you first came in,' said Paddy Breen.

'But he was standing just there.'

Maria looked puzzled and stared at the back of the shop and the place where the boy had been. She went to the corner and looked up the next aisle. It was empty.

The boy had simply vanished.

CHAPTER TWO

Paddy Breen was outside the shop the next morning when Maria arrived with her father. Maria's father was carrying the morning's tray of fresh loaves. Paddy was talking to a carpenter who was on a ladder, doing some repairs to the sign above the door, which said: 'BREEN'S SUPERMARKET'.

Paddy came towards Maria's father, making sure to go around the ladder and not underneath it. He thought it was bad luck to walk under ladders. Paddy was superstitious, and thought lots of things were bad luck, like spilling salt or breaking a mirror or seeing one magpie.

'Morning, Mike,' said Paddy. 'I hope your young helper will be a bit more careful today. No messing with the shelves, eh?'

'But I didn't . . .' Maria began.

'It's all right, Maria,' her father said. 'She'll be no trouble, Paddy.'

Maria glared at Paddy Breen, but said nothing. It was so unfair to be blamed for something she didn't do. If she saw the boy again, she'd tell him off.

And she did see him. When her father went away to get another tray of loaves, the boy was standing in the same place as before, beside the shelves of flour.

But before Maria could speak, he put his finger to his lips. Then he began to move along the shelves at the back of the store. He turned and beckoned her to follow. She hesitated, but then followed him.

Behind the row of shelves against the far wall there was a gap just big enough for someone to squeeze into. The boy edged into it, and moved along between the back of the shelves and the wall. Maria followed, and saw a door in the wall.

To her surprise, she saw the boy step towards it, and then vanish! He seemed to have gone straight through the door without even opening it.

Maria's heart started beating faster. What could be happening? Fearfully, she stretched her hand out to reach the door-knob. She turned it and pushed. With a creak the door opened and she stepped through it.

Maria looked around. She was in a dusty, gloomy room. The only light came from a dirty skylight in the roof. The place was full of old boxes and pieces of broken furniture. Along one wall there was an iron bed with a tattered mattress on it. It looked like an old junk room that no one had used for years.

At first she seemed to be alone, but then Maria saw the boy, standing against the wall. He spread out his hands and, with a shock, Maria heard him speak for the first time:

'This is where I used to live.'

His voice was light and husky, and sounded

almost as if it came from far away.

Maria gazed around. She thought the room looked run down. Imagine living here! As though he read her thoughts, the boy said:

'This was once my own room. That was a long time ago – many years. I loved it back then. There was a window there. He has blocked it up. I had posters on the walls; lots of games, puzzles, records and books. I had friends over all the time. We had fun.'

'So what happened?' Maria asked. Her voice sounded hoarse.

There was a silence. The boy stared hard at her. Then he said:

'We had to leave: our home, our shop, every-thing.'

'This was your family's shop?'

The boy nodded.

'Duff's Grocers. I'm Davy Duff.'

'I'm Maria. Maria O'Malley.'

'I know. I've been watching you, hoping we

might be able to talk.'

'How old are you, Davy?' Maria asked. She was a little startled that Davy knew so much about her.

'I'm nine, the same age as you, Maria.'

Maria gazed at him. Again her heart beat faster. So Davy said he lived here years ago. Yet he had had all those things – games and books, just the kind of things she had now. Maria was afraid to believe it, but it must be true. This was a boy who had lived in another time, but had somehow come back to his old room and his old house. So where was he now? He must be grown-up . . . or had he never grown up at all? That was the creepiest thought of all – his life had stopped at the age of nine. He would be nine years old for ever.

Maria shivered. Davy looked real enough. And yet he seemed to have gone straight through that closed door. And neither her father nor Paddy Breen seemed to have seen him. How come he knew so much about her? Had Davy come back from his other world just to meet *her?* And if so, why?

Just then, Davy said:

'Maria, I need your help.'

CHAPTER THREE

'My help?' Maria asked Davy nervously. 'What for?'

'I want revenge. I want justice for my family and our old home. It's because of Paddy Breen … that I'm … like this. I want to scare him!'

'And your family, your mother and father. Are they …?' Maria hesitated. She was afraid to ask.

'Yes. All gone. Thanks to that rat!' Davy said frowning.

Maria couldn't believe it. However horrible Paddy Breen was, surely he wouldn't commit murder.

'But if he killed you all,' she said, 'he wouldn't be walking around now. He'd be in jail.'

'He didn't need to kill anyone. He just made sure we had to give up the shop. He put tins of rotten food on the shelves and put things in the take-away meals. People started complaining, then they stopped coming to our shop altogether. There was nothing we could do. We couldn't prove anything. In the end my family was desperate. We weren't making any money and owed money to the bank. Paddy Breen offered to buy us out, at a cheap rate. We just had to do it.'

Maria wondered what happened after that, and how Davy and his parents died. But you couldn't just ask someone:

'By the way, how did you die?'

That would sound crazy – but then this whole situation was getting weirder by the minute.

Instead she said:

'No wonder you want revenge, Davy.'

'You'll help, then?' Davy asked with a hopeful smile.

'I don't see what I can do.'

'First, you can help me find the sign.'

'What sign is that?' Maria asked.

'The wooden sign that used to be over the front door. It was green with big gold letters, saying: Duff's Grocers. Paddy Breen took it down and put his own sign up.'

'Perhaps he threw the old sign away,' Maria suggested.

'I don't think so, somehow. Paddy Breen is superstitious. He'd think it was bad luck to throw it out. I'm sure he's hidden it somewhere – maybe in here.'

'Have you looked for it here?' Maria looked around at the boxes and junk piled in the room.

'I've tried, but I can't move anything, you see.' Davy went over to a chair, put his hands out and grasped the arms. He raised his hands to lift it, but they just went straight through the wood.

Maria remembered how she had seen Davy himself go straight through the closed door. She suddenly had a shivery feeling as she stared at the boy. He looked real enough, but Maria knew otherwise. She wondered if she was dreaming it all. She shut her eyes tight and then opened them again. Davy was still there, gazing at her.

'Well?' he said. 'Will you help me?'

'I'll try,' said Maria. She opened a big cardboard box and rummaged among the old papers inside.

'Nothing there,' she said.

She opened another box, then another. One was also full of dusty papers; the other had a pile of clothes in it. They were frayed and moth-eaten. She held them up one by one: there was a pair of shorts, some trousers, a brown coat like the kind shopkeepers used to wear, and a tweed cap with a peak.

'That was my father's,' said Davy in a quiet voice.

Maria held it out to him. But when he took it, his hand just went straight through it and it fell to the floor. Maria picked it up and dusted it. She looked at Davy. He seemed very sad.

Maria tried to think of something to say.

Noticing his bare feet again, she said:

'We haven't found any shoes, Davy. What happened to your shoes?'

Davy looked down at his feet and said:

'Lost in the lake.'

'How? Were you swimming?' Maria asked.

Davy just shook his head slowly. He said no more. Maria felt so sorry for him. She said briskly:

'Come on, let's keep looking for that sign.'

Davy could only watch as she moved boxes, opened a cupboard, and shifted chairs around. She even looked under the bed. Finally Maria stood up, brushing the dust from her clothes. 'I'm sorry, Davy,' she said, 'it's not here.'

'We'll find it,' said Davy, 'but there's something else we need to do.'

'What's that?' asked Maria. 'I'll help you if I can.'

'I want you to write a letter for me,' said Davy. 'A letter to Paddy Breen.'

CHAPTER FOUR

'What do you want me to tell him?' Maria asked. She wasn't sure this was a good idea.

'Tell him I want justice!' cried Davy. 'I want revenge!' he shouted and punched the air, making Maria jump.

Just then, Maria heard her father's voice, out in the shop.

'Maria, where are you? Maria!'

'I've got to go,' she said quickly, still a bit shaken.

'But the letter . . . '

'Tomorrow,' said Maria, going towards the door.

'Tomorrow,' said Davy. 'You promise?'

'I promise.'

Maria opened the door and went back into the shop, and along the narrow passage behind the shelves. She saw her father placing the last loaf on the shelves.

'I'm sorry I was so long, Dad,' Maria said.

Her father looked puzzled.

'Long? What do you mean?' He looked at his watch.

Maria looked at hers. Startled, she realised it said exactly the same time as when she had followed Davy. Yet she thought she must have spent at least twenty minutes with him. How could no time have passed?

'Oh, nothing, Dad.' Maria said

Paddy Breen came up to them and sneered. 'Well, Ms O'Malley, I see you've managed to keep things tidy today. No mess on the floor. Thank you.'

'She's always tidy, Paddy,' Maria's father said sharply.

Maria was annoyed with Paddy Breen and

glared at him. She thought of what Davy had told her, and got even more annoyed.

'Can I ask you something, Mr Breen?' she said.

'Of course. Ask away?'

'Did you ever know a boy called Davy Duff?'

Paddy Breen looked flustered. 'Davy Duff? Was that his name? There was a Duff family here, a long time ago.'

Maria's father laughed.

'Come on, Paddy, is your memory going or what? Didn't you buy the store from the Duffs?'

'Oh, of course, you mean *those* Duffs. Yes, I did. I just didn't remember the boy's name.'

Maria decided to try and test him even more. 'Was there a sign over the door one time, saying: Duff's Grocers?'

'I remember that,' said her father, 'but how did *you* know, Maria? It was years before you were born.'

'I just heard about it somewhere,' said Maria. 'I wonder what happened to the sign?'

'I've no idea!' snapped Paddy Breen. 'What does it matter?'

Maria knew it mattered very much to someone. And Paddy Breen might come to think it mattered too, once he got the letter. She hadn't been sure about Davy's idea of the letter before, but Paddy Breen's replies had made up her mind. He deserved to be scared. Now she was excited at the thought of it. She and Davy would really put the frighteners on him!

CHAPTER FIVE

'I think Paddy Breen's losing it,' Maria's father told her mother as they sat having tea that evening.

'It's a pity he didn't get lost himself,' she replied. 'He's a sleazy creep that one. But how do you mean – losing it?'

'Well, today he couldn't remember the name of the Duffs when Maria asked him about them. I had to remind him he'd bought the shop from them.'

'And there was something a bit shady about that deal, so people said. There were even rumours that he'd messed with the food so customers would stop coming, and the Duffs would have to sell quickly and at a low price.'

'Yes, they were rumours,' Maria's father was cautious, 'but nothing was ever proved.'

'What happened to the Duffs after they sold the supermarket?' Maria asked.

'It's a tragic story,' said her mother. 'They managed to find a small, run-down old house, over on the far side of the lake, and they were going to live there, and do it up. They were going over there in a boat when a storm blew up. The boat capsized and they all drowned.'

'Mike and Mary Duff are buried in the churchyard here in town,' said Maria's father.

'And Davy?' asked Maria softly.

'His body was never found. They searched the lake for days, but there was no sign of him.'

'He was their only child,' said Maria's mother. 'It was such a tragedy.'

'Had they any other family?'

'Not that I know of, but someone told me they heard that Mr Duff's aunt lived in a cottage just outside the town.'

Maria decided to see what she could find out about the family. At school they were doing a local history project. They had to go and talk to old people and write down their memories of the old days and how people lived. Maybe she could track down Davy's relative, and find out more about the Duffs. What relation would she be to Davy? Maria worked out that she would be his great-aunt. Perhaps Davy would know where she was. She would ask him tomorrow.

* * *

'Auntie Lily, that's what Mam and Dad called her,' said Davy the next day, as they stood in the store room. 'She asked me to call her Lily. She said calling her Great-Aunt Lily would make her feel ancient.'

'What was she like?'

'Fun and lively. She used to make us great teas with cream cakes and all. Her cottage was out in the country. She worked in the pet-food factory in town. She drove in every day in a rusty old car. My father said one day it would fall to bits under her and leave her sitting on the road!'

'Was she married?'

'For a while, but I never met her husband.

They split up. Just as well, my parents said. They said he was a "bad lot", whatever that means. They never had any children.'

'I'd like to meet her.'

'I don't know if she's still around. But I could show you where she used to live.'

'Great. If she's still there, I can talk to her about her memories for our school history project. But first, we've got work to do.'

'The letter!'

'Right. I've brought some paper and a pen. A dark-red felt pen. Perhaps Paddy will think it's written in blood!'

'Fantastic. We can put a skull and crossbones on it.'

'But that's for pirates, isn't it?

'Never mind, it looks frightening.'

'Skull and crossbones it is!' Maria took the paper and pen out of her pocket and knelt down beside a big wooden box. She spread the paper on it, and Davy stood looking over her shoulder, as she began to draw.

'You're an artist!' he said, as he watched Maria draw a big skull with hollow eyes and a toothy grin, and two crossed bones underneath.

Thanks, Davy,' said Maria. 'Now, what message shall we write?'

What about, *BEWARE! THE DUFFS ARE HERE!'*

'Or maybe, *FEAR, FEAR! THE DUFFS ARE HERE!'*

'Maria, you're a poet as well!' said Davy.

They laughed as Maria began to write.

CHAPTER SIX

'There – it's finished!' said Maria, holding up the letter. Davy looked at it and smiled. Maria had written the message in big capital letters, and put some dots around the letters, hoping they would look like spots of blood.

'*FEAR, FEAR! THE DUFFS ARE HERE!*' Davy read out.

'Great work, Maria! That should scare Paddy Breen, he'll be ready to do whatever we want, and then I can get revenge for what he did to my family.'

Maria wasn't sure Paddy would scare so easily. She asked:

'What do we want him to do?'

'Change the name of the shop for a start,' said Davy, 'back to Duff's Grocers. That's why we must find the old sign.'

'And what then?'

'We've got to frighten him so much that he thinks the shop is haunted.'

'Well, it's true, isn't it?' Maria smiled. 'Here you are to prove it.'

Davy laughed.

'Yes, you're right. And I'm sure he'd be really spooked if he saw me. The trouble is he can't. No one was able to see me or hear me either. I could jump up and down making blood-curdling screams in the aisles, but I might as well have been a million miles away, for all the notice anyone took of me. That is until you came along, Maria.'

'But how is it that *I'm* able to see you?'

'I don't know – I guess it's a mystery. I was hoping you might, and the other day, I just suddenly realised you could. You must have some kind of extra sense. There are people who do. They can make a bridge between their world and ours.'

Maria felt strange. She had that intense cold, shivery feeling again. She wasn't sure she wanted to have this extra sense that Davy talked about. It was a lot of fun meeting Davy and planning to outwit Paddy Breen. But supposing she got sucked in more and more to *his* world, as Davy called it. She wondered what would happen if she tore the letter up and said she wouldn't go on with the plan.

She looked at Davy, as he stared at the letter she had written for him and grinned.

'Thanks, Maria,' he said. 'You're a real friend.'

She couldn't let him down now. She'd go on. She was too excited to know what would happen, to give up now.

'Thanks, Davy,' she said. 'You too.'

She put up her hand in a high-five gesture. Davy smiled, raised his own hand and went to slap the palm against hers. But Davy's hand went right through her own, and as it did, Maria got a freezing-cold sensation.

He smiled sheepishly.

'Sorry,' he said, 'I forgot for a moment.'

'That was strange,' she said.

'What?'

She told him about the cold feeling when their hands met. He looked sad.

Maria smiled.

'Friends it is, anyway, Davy. But now we've got to work something out.'

'Yes?'

'Yes. What are we going to do with the letter?'

'I've got a great idea,' said Davy. 'Could you slip it into one of your father's loaves while they're baking? Then it would be a message like a fortune cookie!'

Maria laughed. 'A great idea, but I'm not sure it would survive the oven. And how could we make sure Paddy Breen got the loaf himself? Some customer might cut into it at home, and complain about my father's baking.'

'You could slip the letter into his pocket.'

'It's too risky. You know what — I think we should post it! He won't have any idea who sent it. He'll be really worried. Then we can think up more ways of scaring him.'

'Right so, the post it is.'

'I'll do it today. With any luck it will arrive first thing in the morning.'

'I can hardly wait.'

'Nor me. Hey, I've just thought of something we can do. This afternoon, why don't you bring me out to your Aunt Lily's. I'll bring my bike.'

'That's terrific. I'll meet you just outside town, beside the petrol station.'

'Okay, I'll be there at three o'clock.'

* * *

Just before three, Maria leaned her bike against the low wall just past the petrol station. On the way there she had stopped at the post box and posted the letter. She had her notebook, her digital camera and tape-recorder in her ruck-sack in the basket of her bike. She just hoped that Davy's great-aunt was still alive, and still living in the cottage.

A big blue car drew up and pulled into the petrol station. It parked just inside the entrance to the forecourt where the pumps were. A big man got out and looked around. It was Paddy Breen. Before Maria could move away, he looked up the road and saw her.

CHAPTER SEVEN

Maria remembered that Paddy Breen owned this petrol station as well as the supermarket. She wondered if he had swindled somebody else to get that.

Paddy called out:

'Well, hello Maria! You seem to be turning up everywhere these days. Are you following me like a private eye?'

Maria decided not to answer back and to be polite. She would wait, and enjoy Paddy's reaction when he got the letter tomorrow.

'Hello, Mr Breen,' she called. 'I was just out for a bike ride.'

'You won't need any petrol, then?' said Paddy Breen sarcastically.

'I guess not,' Maria smiled.

'Then you can stop sitting on the wall of my petrol station.'

Maria was furious, but she didn't show it. She jumped off the wall and grabbed her bike.

'I'm sorry Mr Breen,' she said. 'I didn't realise it was for customers only.'

Paddy Breen just glared at her. Then he grunted, turned and walked away towards the petrol station.

'No manners, that's his problem.'

Maria was startled to hear Davy's voice just behind her. She turned around.

'Hi there!' he said.

'Hi, Davy,' said Maria.

'Shall we head for Auntie Lily's? I'll come some of the way with you.'

'Why not the whole way? I could do with a bit of encouragement.'

Davy looked sad. 'I've tried to get there, often, but after a couple of hundred metres, my powers seem to sort of fade out.'

'Maybe this time you'll make it to the cottage.'

'Let's hope so. Come on, I'll run beside you.'

Maria got on her bike and began to pedal along slowly so that Davy could keep up.

'You can go faster,' he said.

So Maria pedalled faster. Davy seemed to be falling behind, but he said:

'Carry on, Maria, I'll be fine.'

She went on pedalling fast, looking at the road in front. Suddenly, Davy's figure appeared, about ten metres ahead, running fast. He turned and waved, then went on running. She overtook him, and he told her to keep cycling. He fell behind then suddenly appeared again in front of her. After a while he stopped, and she caught up with him. She stopped too, and got off the bike.

'Are you all right, Davy?'

He seemed to be gasping for breath. Then Maria realised with a shock that his whole face was getting fainter, and so were his clothes. He was slowly vanishing before her eyes.

'I'm sorry, Maria, it's happening again. I can't go any further.' Davy's voice was getting weaker. 'Go on past the crossroads. You'll see the cottage at the edge of the field, on the left. If I can, I'll wait for you on the way back, near the petrol station. Good luck.' He raised his arm limply in a wave. Then he disappeared altogether.

Maria felt a sudden chill come over her and she shivered. Then she grabbed the handlebars and got on the bike. She pedalled as hard as she could. It wasn't long before she reached the crossroads. She got off her bike. On the far side of the crossroads she could see a field on the left, and a cottage standing on its own behind a straggly hedge. The cottage was made of stone, and had an old, green door, which needed a new lick of paint. There was a window on each side of the door, and a slate roof with a number of missing slates.

Maria wheeled her bike over the crossroads and leaned it against the hedge, beside the broken gate. The tiny garden was neglected and overgrown. This didn't look very hopeful. The place seemed as if it was deserted.

Maria went up the path and knocked twice on the door using the rusty metal knocker.

She waited. There was no sound, only the wind rustling in the bushes. The sky was a heavy grey colour and it looked like it would rain soon. Maria knocked again. She put her ear against the door. After a while she heard shuffling footsteps inside. Her heart was beating fast, as the footsteps approached. She heard a key turn in the lock, and then with a creaking sound the door opened slowly.

CHAPTER EIGHT

Inside the door stood a big woman in a dark-green dress with a white collar. She had grey hair with frizzy curls, and glasses that hung on a cord around her neck.

'Hello,' she said, with an air of surprise.

'Hello,' said Maria. 'I was looking for Mrs Lily Duff.'

'That's me,' said the woman, 'though Marsh is my married name. Are you collecting for a charity?'

'No, I'm doing a school project for St Mary's National School. My name is Maria O'Malley. I wonder if I could talk to you for a few minutes?' Maria said producing a letter from her school about the project.

'Of course. Come in.' Mrs Marsh led the way through a small, dark hallway into a sitting

room. crammed with furniture and ornaments. There were lots of chairs and small tables, all piled with books and newspapers. Two big armchairs stood on either side of a brick fireplace with framed photographs on the mantelpiece. One was of a smiling couple in a garden – a boy in shorts stood between them. Maria saw with a shock that the boy was Davy.

'Do sit down, Maria,' said Mrs Marsh, pointing to one of the armchairs. She sat down opposite and listened as Maria told her that they were collecting stories from older people about what life was like when they were young.

'Well, I'll do my best to help you,' said Mrs Marsh, 'but you might find my life rather ordinary, I'm afraid.'

'Oh, it's the ordinary things that are interesting,' Maria said eagerly, 'like what games you played when you were children, before there were PlayStations and such, and what kind of food you liked . . .'

'I'll be happy to tell you anything you want to know, just ask away.'

Maria took her notebook and pen out, and put her tape-recorder on the table between them.

'You're a very efficient reporter,' Mrs Marsh. 'Maybe you'll work for a newspaper one day.'

Maria smiled. That was exactly the sort of career she dreamed about. 'Thank you,' she said, 'Now first of all . . .'

***

Mrs Marsh talked about growing up in the town, her schooldays and the strict rules they had. Then she talked about the job she had helping her brother in the grocery shop and then getting the job in the pet-food factory.

'The grocery shop,' said Maria. 'That would be Duff's Grocers, where Breen's Supermarket is now?'

'That's right – you've certainly done your research well.'

'My father is a baker; he supplies bread to Breen's every day. I help him during the holidays.'

'Of course – O'Malley's Bakery. So that's your family's business. I remember your father as a young lad, long ago. He used to help his father, just like you do now.'

'What was the shop like when it was Duff's Grocers?'

'It was really more of a corner shop originally, but after my brother died, his son and his wife took it over. They were wonderful. They worked so hard, and everyone liked them. They were able to expand. It was a real success story, until …'

'Until someone started tampering with the food.'

'How do you know about that?' asked Mrs Marsh sharply.

'Oh, I just heard some rumours.' said Maria.

'Well, I'd advise you not to go spreading them around. It could get you into trouble. Besides, it's too late now for the family. We can't bring any of them back. They're all gone – all three of them. It will be the anniversary soon: just twenty years since that terrible day.'

Mrs Marsh was gazing at the photograph on the mantelpiece. She started to cry quietly. Maria was more determined than ever to help Davy to get revenge.

'I'm sorry,' said Maria. 'Is that them, in the photo?'

'That's right.' Mrs Marsh sighed.

Maria stood up and looked at the picture in the frame. Davy's father had long hair, and an open-neck shirt. His mother's hair was curly, and she was wearing a smart dress with a white collar. Between them, Davy stood with his hands on his hips, grinning at the camera. It was exactly like the eager smile he still had now.

Lily said:

'They were a lovely family, and Davy was a great boy, full of fun and fantastic schemes. He was about your age. You'd have liked him.'

'I'm sure I would,' Maria smiled.

'It's strange, when I see him smiling out at me there in the picture, I almost feel as if he hadn't drowned at all, that his presence is still around, and he might walk in the door any minute.' She sighed again.

Maria felt herself shiver. She glanced towards the door, half expecting to see Davy appear. But there was nothing there. She sat down again.

Mrs Marsh went on:

'It seems so unfair, the younger generations dying first. Now there's only me left, and I may not be here for that long. Well, not in this house, anyway.'

'You're going to move?'

'I'll have to. I just got a letter yesterday, saying the landlord wants to put up the rent. I won't be able to afford it.'

Maria saw her glance at some papers that were on the table. She saw the top one was a letter with a printed heading saying PJB ESTATES. Mrs Marsh was frowning.

Then she looked up at Maria and said:

'Anyway, this isn't any help to your project. What else would you like to know?'

Maria asked a few more questions, then took a photo of Mrs Marsh with her digital camera, and asked if she could take one of the family portraits on the mantelpiece.

'Certainly,' she said. 'It would be good to have them remembered in your project.'

* * *

Maria cycled back towards the town. She was thinking sadly about Mrs Marsh and all she had been through. She wished there was some way she could help her, and then she thought maybe there was. Excited by her idea, Maria pedalled faster. She would talk about it with Davy, if he was there. She just hoped he'd be beside the road where he had said.

CHAPTER NINE

As Maria turned the corner, the road into town stretched ahead. There was nobody beside the road near the petrol station. Disappointed, she rode on towards it. Suddenly, when she was about fifty metres from the petrol station, she saw the figure of Davy appear, sitting on the wall. He looked towards her and waved. Maria stopped beside him.

She told him all about her meeting with Lily, and the photograph on the mantelpiece, and how she might have to leave because of the landlord putting up the rent.

'Where will she go?' Davy asked.

'I don't know. She seemed pretty hard up, I thought.'

'It's outrageous!' Davy was angry. 'We've got

to stop it. But what can we do?'

'I know where we can start. I saw the land-lord's name on the letter: PJB ESTATES. Let's go to the library and look it up on the Internet.'

***

In the library, Maria sat at the computer while Davy hovered behind her. She soon found a register of property owners in the town, and scrolled down the screen.

'There it is!' she cried. 'PJB ESTATES!'

She realised that several people near her were looking at her because she was talking. They thought she was on her own. Maria forgot that only she could see Davy.

She smiled sweetly at them, as Davy said: 'Look what it says!'

Maria gazed at the screen. She read:

PJB ESTATES: PROPERTY.

CHAIRMAN & CHIEF EXECUTIVE:

PATRICK JEREMIAH BREEN.

'Paddy Breen!' Maria said softly.

'We're going to get him, Maria,' said Davy grimly. 'There's no way I'll let him turn Lily out of her home.'

'Roll on tomorrow,' Maria whispered, 'when Patrick Jeremiah Breen gets our letter!'

* * *

Next morning when Maria arrived in the shop with her father, Paddy was chatting with Rose. Rose looked bored and Paddy was cheerful. Maria guessed the post couldn't have come yet. When it did, he would not be so calm and cheerful!

Davy appeared, and beckoned her. She followed him into the old store-room.

'I've been thinking,' said Davy. 'The letter won't be enough to scare Paddy Breen. We must do more. You see that pile of old newspapers under the bed? There might be one with the report of our accident on the lake.'

'Nearly twenty years ago.'

'That's right. It will be twenty years ago on Wednesday.'

'It must have been big news, all right,' said Maria, dragging the pile of papers out and looking through them. They were dusty and faded. Finally Maria found some from the right year – twenty years ago.

'What was the date of the accident?' she asked.

'The twentieth of July.'

'So it would have been in the paper the next day . . . Here it is!' Maria held up the old paper.

Davy knelt down beside her. They read the headline: FAMILY DROWNED IN BOAT TRAGEDY

There was a description of the accident, and eyewitness accounts by people on the shore, and by those in other boats who had gone out to try and help. The report told how the bodies of Davy's parents had been dragged from the water, but there was no sign of Davy's.

'I'm so sorry, Davy,' said Maria tearfully.

'I know, thank you. We can use this to help scare

Paddy, if we could only make some copies ... '

'There's bound to be a photocopier in Paddy's office at the back of the shop. Maybe I can sneak in and make copies there.'

Maria went back into the shop. Again, it seemed that no time had passed. Paddy was still at the front, talking to Rose and looking at her till receipts. Maria's father was loading the shelves with bread. She went quietly down the short corridor at the back of the store, and opened the office door. A photocopier was in the corner.

It didn't take Maria long to make several copies of the old paper. She folded them and put them in her rucksack.

She was just going back to the door when she noticed the computer at the side of Paddy Breen's desk. She remembered the picture of the family photograph she had taken at the cottage, and had an idea.

She took the card from the digital camera and

put it into the computer. Soon she had the photo of Davy and his parents enlarged on the screen. That should really put the wind up Paddy! She took out one of the newspaper photocopies and laid it down on the desk beside the computer.

***

Back in the room, Davy was delighted.

'We'll put the other copies around the shelves where people will come across them. What are you doing?'

Maria was kneeling down and rummaging under the bed.

'Davy, what's this? It's a box,' Maria said as she pulled a heavy box from under the bed. 'Oh look, look, it's got some old tins in it!'

Davy gasped as he leant over the box. The tins were old and rusty, but as Maria picked them up she could just read the faded labels. There were baked beans, tins of tomatoes, mushy peas and tinned tuna. She showed them to Davy.

'Just a minute!' he said excitedly. 'Show me the

top of that one again.' He peered at it closely and cried: 'Maria, I think we've found the evidence to nail Paddy Breen once and for all!'

CHAPTER TEN

'Nail Paddy Breen? How?' asked Maria.

'See the top of that tin? If you look closely you can see a hole in the top, just near the side, and another one opposite.'

'Yes, like it was made by a small nail.' Maria said, getting excited.

'You see, somebody taking that off the shelf when it was new wouldn't notice. But with air getting into the tin, whatever's inside would go bad quite soon.' Davy explained.

'And when it was opened, YUK!' Maria wrinkled up her nose.

'Paddy must have been regularly piercing tins and putting them in among the good ones. Nobody realised they'd been messed with. They just thought my parents were selling rotten goods.'

'And they stopped shopping here.'

'That's right,' said Davy. 'This box of tins must have been one he'd started using, and then forgot about, after his plan succeeded. Of course there's no smell now, the stuff inside will have long dried up and crumbled away. This box of tins is our evidence!'

'So what's your plan now?'

'If you can secretly put some of these old tins around the shop on different shelves, customers will soon start complaining. And when Paddy sees the tins, he'll know he's been found out, and he'll think the Duffs have come back to haunt him.'

'Well, one of them *has!* Maria grinned.

'Yes, indeed.' Davy smiled.

***

Maria wandered around the shop, putting the photocopies and the tins on various shelves. Innocently, she strolled past Paddy at the check-out, and went outside. The carpenter was at the top of the ladder, taking away some of the wood above the shop sign, to repair it. Maria stopped and looked up, and noticed that Davy was beside her. He pointed.

'That's where our sign was, up there,' he said. 'It hung from two short chains, just where that gap is. I'll show you.'

Davy climbed up the ladder behind the carpenter. He leaned out and pointed to the gap. Then he climbed down again and stood beside Maria. He was very excited.

'It's there!' he said. 'The sign is still there!'

'What do you mean?'

'It must have been lifted and pushed in behind the new boarding they put up. I could see the edge of it.'

He asked Maria to call up to the carpenter and ask was there anything hidden in the gap. The carpenter laughed, but decided to humour her.

'You're right, girl! There *is* something there!' the carpenter said with a surprised laugh.

He tugged at the heavy piece of wood. It clattered down, nearly knocking him off the ladder. He jumped clear. The sign was still held by its chains, and just fell a short way until it stopped. They all looked up.

It was a long rectangle of green wood, with gold letters on it, saying: DUFF'S GROCERS. The carpenter decided to take a tea break to recover. Maria and Davy punched the air in triumph. They were just admiring the sign when the postman stopped his bike outside the door of the shop, and went inside with a bundle of letters.

'The letter!' said Davy and Maria together, as they followed him in.

Paddy was too busy to take any notice of the postman. He was standing beside Rose at the check-out, with a piece of paper in his hand. It was one of the photocopies of the newspaper article that Maria left around the shop.

The postman said:

'Here's your post, Paddy,' and put it down beside him on the counter.

'Thanks,' Paddy muttered, and went on staring at the paper. He glared at Rose and barked:

'Where did you get this?'

'I told you,' Rose was impatient. 'It was there beside the till.'

'You did it yourself!' Paddy Breen snapped. 'It's some kind of sick joke, isn't it?'

'Don't be stupid! I've got better things to do than play tricks on you,' Rose snapped.

Maria saw Paddy glare around the shop – so she dodged behind some shelves.

'I'll find out, I'll find out!' he snarled. Maria peered out and saw him riffle through the bundle of letters.

'Bills, bills, bills!' he grumbled. Then he stopped. He was looking at the spidery dark-red writing on Maria's envelope. He tore it open and took out the letter.

CHAPTER ELEVEN

Maria thought Paddy Breen was going to explode. His hand shook as he gripped the letter and stared at it. His face went red and he began cursing under his breath.

'Mind your language, Paddy,' said Rose. 'There are customers around.' Rose was right – some of the customers nearby were staring at him.

'Well done, Maria,' whispered Davy beside her.

Paddy just stood still.

'The Duffs!' he said, glowering.

'Calm down, Paddy,' said Rose. 'The Duffs are dead, long ago.'

Davy winked at Maria, and went quickly across to the check-out counter and stood behind Paddy Breen. Maria saw Davy brush his hand to and fro across the back of Paddy's neck. Maria had remembered how cold *she* had felt when Davy's hand touched hers.

It worked. Paddy shivered, and looked around uneasily. He gazed at the letter again, then suddenly crumpled it into a ball, and shouted:

'I've got it! There's only one person who could be doing this!'

'Paddy, quiet!' said Rose sharply, as the customers looked startled.

Davy was back beside Maria. They looked at each other in alarm. They were both afraid Paddy might attack her, guessing that she was the culprit.

'I'd better make myself scarce!' she whispered, turning to go.

But Paddy, clutching the letter, went stomping up the aisle past them towards his office. As he passed they heard him say furiously:

'Lily Marsh! Lily Marsh!'

'Wow!' said Davy. 'He thinks Lily organised all this.'

'Oh no, this could make it worse for Lily,' said Maria.

'Paddy must be going to ring her,' said Davy. 'I'll go in and hear what he says.'

'Okay, I'll wait for you in your old room,' said Maria excitedly.

Maria watched Davy follow Paddy Breen up the corridor, and when he slammed the door behind him, Davy walked straight through it.

***

A few minutes later, Davy joined Maria in the room.

'Paddy went crazy,' he said. 'He was shouting and swearing at Lily on the phone, and saying he didn't know how she'd done it, but he knew she had organised it all to scare him.'

'I wonder what she said.'

'I was able to lean close to the receiver and

listen,' said Davy. 'Lily was very brave. She said Paddy must be going mad and he'd imagined it all. It must be his guilty conscience, and the past was coming back to haunt him.'

'*Haunt* is right.'

'Yes, he was shaken by that word all right, especially as I started stroking his neck again and his bald head too! By the end of the call, he was shivering and shaking like jelly. He shouted at Lily that he was going to get her and turn her out on the street. Lily just said he was crazy, and hung up.'

* * *

When they came back into the shop, Paddy Breen was striding down the aisle, he was flushed and muttering. The customers were giving him very odd glances. Just as he reached the front of the shop, he met the carpenter coming in.

'Paddy, come and take a look at this,' he said.

'Not now, not now. What is it?' Paddy asked impatiently.

'Come out and see.'

Paddy Breen was very flustered as he followed the carpenter out to the front of the shop. Maria and Davy followed Paddy outside, just in time to see him staring up at the sign and shouting at the carpenter and raising his fist. The carpenter shouted back, and grabbed hold of Paddy's wrist. Maria saw Davy suddenly appear behind Paddy, and stroke his neck. Paddy shuddered, dropped his arm and hurried back into the shop.

He was just in time to see Rose at the check-out counter having a row with a customer, a big red-faced woman in a green cardigan, who was holding up one of the rusty old tins.

'What kind of a shop do you call this?' she asked. 'Trying to palm us off with something you dug up from the ground, by the look of it.'

An old man with a cap and a tweed coat said:

'Yeah, I'd say that's passed its sell-by-date, all right!'

Customers nearby laughed.

'It's not funny!' said a large woman in a flowery dress, holding a chubby smiling toddler. She held up another rusty tin. 'You could poison people with this.'

'Well, here's the man to ask about it.,' said Rose, pointing at Paddy Breen. All the customers turned on him, holding out the tins and shouting.

Paddy Breen took one of the tins. He went

very pale, and his eyes flickered from side to side.

'Where did you get these?' he asked in a low voice.

'Off your shelves – you chancer!' snapped the big woman.

'And look, there's another one!' said the old man in the cap, pointing to a shelf nearby. Paddy Breen seized the tin. He stared at the top of it, and opened his mouth to speak, but no words came out. He just stood there, gulping like a goldfish.

'We should get the Guards, it's a criminal offence to sell goods in that state!' said the woman with the toddler.

'Yes, the Guards!' chorused the other customers.

'No, no, we don't need the Guards!' Paddy was sweating now. 'I'll sort this out. There'll be compensation for everyone. Just wait a moment.'

Still clutching the tin, he hurried back into the office. Davy followed.

CHAPTER TWELVE

Maria went into Davy's old room. Davy came back in a few minutes, very excited.

'I can't believe it, I can't believe it!' he cried.

'What's happened?'

'Paddy rang Lily again. He's totally spooked by the whole thing, and afraid he'll be found out. He's promised not to put up her rent. In fact he even said he'd decorate the house for her, and let her live there as long as she wants, rent-free.'

'He must think she knows all about what he did to put your family out of the business,' said Maria.

'But he's still got the business,' Davy looked grim.

'Maybe we can do something about that,' Maria smiled.

'What do you mean?'

'I've got an idea. Follow me.'

Maria led him back into the shop. They could see Paddy frantically going up and down the shelves, trying to find more hidden tins, and grabbing the photocopies.

Maria picked up a photocopy and boldly went up to Paddy and said innocently:

'Mr Breen, can I say something?' She held out the photocopy.

Paddy snatched it and snapped:

'Not now, girl! Can't you see I'm busy?'

But Maria went on:

'It's just that I noticed the date on that article. It's exactly twenty years tomorrow since the accident happened.'

'Yes, yes, what about it?' said Paddy impatiently. But he seemed to go a bit pale.

'The anniversary,' said Maria sweetly. 'Imagine. Davy would have been twenty-nine now.'

'I suppose so,' Paddy muttered. Then he let

out a shriek. Davy had come up behind him and was running his hand across Paddy's neck and head.

'What's wrong, Paddy?' called Rose from the check-out.

'He doesn't look well at all,' said one of the customers.

Paddy was clutching a shelf to steady himself.

'I … I'll be all right in a minute,' he said.

Maria beckoned to Davy. She led him down the aisle towards the office. They slipped inside. Soon, Maria had the picture of Davy and his parents up on the computer screen again. She began to type.

When Davy looked over her shoulder, he saw that under the picture in big black letters, Maria had written:

TWENTY YEARS TOO MANY!

TIME TO GO! TIME TO GO … OR ELSE …

Davy laughed, delighted.

'You're the greatest, Maria!' he cried.

'Let's go and leave him to find it!' said Maria.

They left the office and looked down the aisle, where Paddy was now sitting on a stool Rose had brought for him. She was giving him a glass of water.

As they saw Paddy get up unsteadily, they hid behind the nearest stack of shelves. Peering round, they saw Paddy walk slowly up the aisle, staggering a little. He opened the office door and went in.

Soon afterwards, there was a loud scream from inside the office, then another. Then they heard Paddy cry:

'No! No! No! I give in, I give in!'

They heard a large crash as Paddy pushed the computer off the desk. He flung open the door and stumbled down the aisle and out of the shop.

Davy turned to Maria and gave the thumbs-up sign. Maria punched the air and grinned.

***

Later that day, Maria took her bike and rode out

to Lily's cottage. She knocked several times, but there was no one there.

When she got back home, she was amazed to see that Lily Marsh was in the sitting room with Maria's parents.

They were both smiling happily. So was Mrs Marsh.

'We've got the most amazing news, Maria!' said her mother. 'Mrs Marsh is the new owner of Paddy Breen's supermarket!'

'And Mrs Marsh wants us to run it for her!' exclaimed her father.

'I can hardly believe it all,' said Mrs Marsh. 'I know you'll do a great job.

* * *

Maria couldn't wait to see Davy, who had stayed at the shop to keep an eye on things.

'Paddy's in the office with a lawyer,' he said, 'drawing up the papers for the handover.'

Maria told him about the meeting at her house.

'That's marvellous,' said Davy. 'Lily deserves it all.'

'The Duffs are back in town!' said Maria.

'Here to stay!' said Davy.

'That's what I was wondering,' Maria said. '*Can* you stay, now that things are all sorted out, and you've got your revenge?'

'I hope so,' said Davy.

But Maria noticed that something strange was happening. Davy seemed to be fading.

'Don't go,' said Maria. 'We're friends now. We can't say goodbye.'

'Then we won't,' said Davy. His voice was getting faint. 'I'll make sure to come and see you some time. I just hope that you'll be able to see me.'

'I will – I'm sure of it!' said Maria, as Davy slowly faded and eventually disappeared.

'I *must* be able to,' she said, to convince herself. Then she went towards the door, saying firmly:

'After all, the DUFFS ARE BACK IN TOWN!'

She was sure she heard Davy's echoing voice somewhere in the distance, saying:

'Thank you, Maria, thank you!'